Mummy, Did You Miss Me?

by Judy Hindley

illustrated by Jane Massey

Alice Bear was leaving.

"Where are you going, little one?"
asked Mummy Bear.
"I'm going to find a jungle full of
tigers," said Alice Bear. "Or perhaps
a great big mountain I can climb.
Or perhaps I'll sail across the sea!"

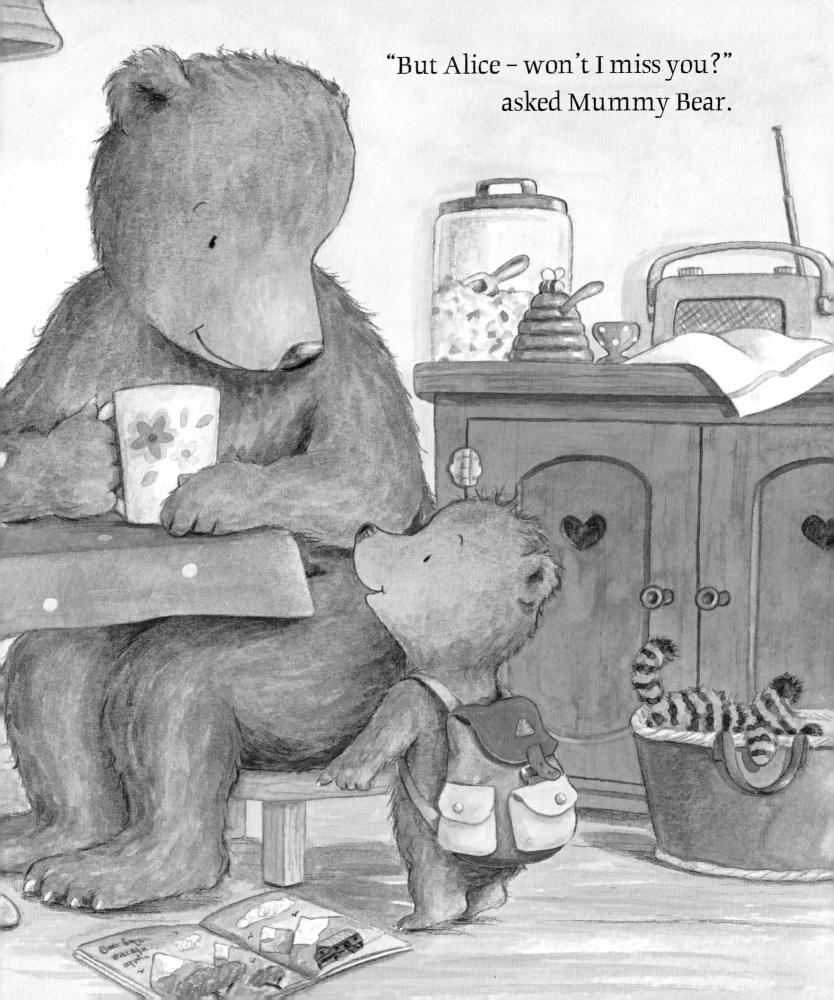

"But Alice – won't I miss you?"
asked Mummy Bear.

"You might miss me a bit," said Alice Bear.
"But you have Arthur. And you have Jenny."

Mummy Bear said, "I like Arthur and Jenny. But they're not you. I'm afraid I'm really going to miss you."

"Oh, don't worry, Mummy Bear," said Alice Bear.
"I'll be home again before you know it!"
Then off she went, and Mummy Bear got busy.

Soon, Mummy Bear went out into the garden.
"Where are you, Alice Bear?" she called.
"I've just thought of such a funny joke!"
But nobody answered her.

"Oh yes," said Mummy Bear.
"My little bear is off on her adventures.
Perhaps she's in a jungle full of tigers!
Well, Jenny, I'll have to tell my joke to you:
Jenny, why don't bears wear shoes?
Because they have to have bear feet."

Then Mummy Bear began to sing. But soon she stopped and called, "Alice Bear! I've just remembered a great song!"

But once again, nobody answered her.
"Oh, no!" said Mummy Bear. "My little bear is still away."

"The bear went over the mountain –
to see what he could see!"

"I'll have to sing my song to Arthur."

"Arthur, just think," she said. "Alice Bear might be on a mountain right this minute. She might be higher than an eagle's nest – higher than the clouds!"

"She'll be able to see far, far away!"

At lunchtime, Mummy Bear put out a picnic. She called her little bear, but nobody answered her except the birds.

"Goodness!" she cried. "That bear is still not home! Maybe she's in a boat, way out at sea. Maybe she'll catch a fish for lunch."

"Never mind – perhaps the birds will eat this."

And guess what?
Someone did eat that lunch!

Was it the birds?

Mummy Bear kept thinking of things to share
with Alice Bear. She found a story for her –
she had to read it to Arthur and Jenny.

She had a job for her – she
saved it for later.

At last she said, "Alice Bear
has been away a long, long time.
I really miss her. And it's time
to go down to the shops.

Who will keep me company
and help me? I need that bear now!"

And just then, who do you think she saw?

"Alice Bear!" cried Mummy Bear.

"You're home!"

"I'm here!"

cried Alice Bear.

"I'm back!"

Then she gave her mummy
the most ENORMOUS hug.
"I was gone a long,
long time," said Alice Bear.
"Did you miss me a little bit?"

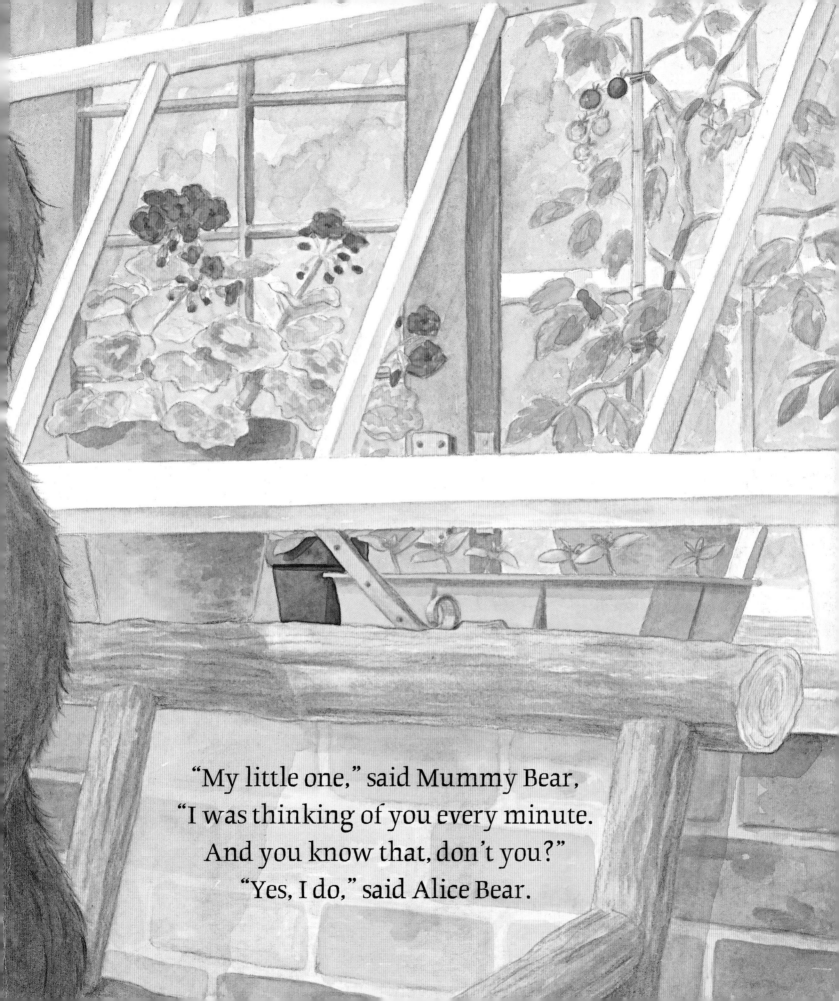

"My little one," said Mummy Bear,
"I was thinking of you every minute.
And you know that, don't you?"
"Yes, I do," said Alice Bear.

And then she told her mummy about
ALL her great adventures.